DUNCAN DARES

TO MIFFINS

First published in Great Britain in 1987 by
Boxtree Limited
25 Floral Street, London WC2E 9DS

ISBN 1 85283 004 2

Designed by Groom & Pickerill
Typeset by York House Typographic Ltd.
Printed by New Interlitho.
The author and publishers would like to thank Donna Bailey for her help in the preparation of this book.
Published by arrangement with BBC Books, a division of BBC Enterprises Limited.

Acknowledgements
I should like to thank Rob Benfield, Alex Leger, Edward Barnes, Roy Thompson, Biddy Baxter, Susie Bryant, Peter Sofroniou, Jenny White, all the BBC Film & Sound Crews, Film Editors, and many others who contributed to the programmes, Geoffrey Hamilton-Fairley, Annie Francis, Tim Condren, Doug Scott, Steve Good, The Marines, Brian Androse, Lofty Wiseman, Ken Beaver, Jim Beales, Horace Jessop, and the T45 Team Tamara Coco's circus, Gandeys Circus, Hang Gliders everywhere and my Guardian Angels.

Photo Credits
Thanks to: Daily Mirror – C. Paterson, Radio Times, A. Chapman, Rob Benfield, BBC Enterprises, Peter Sofroniou, Alex Leger, Paul Wood, Truck and Driver, Steve Chubb, FF Publishing, Bruce Coleman Ltd., Royal Marines.

CONTENTS

INTRODUCTION

Dear Readers,

If you have watched **Duncan Dares** I hope you will enjoy this book about the different things I have tried. Some of these dares were my own ideas, some were suggested by my producers at the BBC and some were suggestions from viewers. They all involved a lot of skill and training and I am grateful to the many people who helped me acquire the necessary skills for some of the dares. I had to push myself to extremes of physical and mental endurance, but the excitement and need to make a good film carried me through from surviving in the wilderness to driving the Water Beetle across the Irish Sea to walking over bed of red hot coals.

One very important thing to remember, both when watching **Duncan Dares** on television or reading about the dares in the book, that YOU SHOULD NEVER ATTEMPT TO COPY ME. Most of the exploits took a lot of practice and I always had skilled experts to help me stay in one piece. But if you've dreamed of climbing Everest or want to be really good at a sport or hobby, you should join a sports club or organisation where you can be properly supervised.

WATER BEETLE

In 1961 three men tried to drive a Volkswagen Beetle across the English Channel. Half way across they sank. My friend Steve Good and I decided to repeat the adventure, but because the English Channel is too crowded for safety, we decided to cross from Stranraer in Scotland to Larne in Northern Ireland, a much rougher sea than the Channel.

After months of preparation, early one overcast morning we made our first attempt. I went up the headland at Stranraer to look at the sea. It was then I realised the dangers of what I was about to do. We had no guarantee the car would stay afloat; the waves outside the loch were big and choppy, and I knew one big wave could turn us over.

A small crowd waved us off as we drove gently down the ramp into the cold waters of Loch Ryan. Only a few feet from the shore, disaster struck and the engine stopped dead. We tried to start it up again, but it was

Left: Our first attempt – doomed!
Above: The Beetle takes to the water. Will we make it?

hopeless. Reluctantly, I waved the life-raft over to tow us ashore. Our first attempt had ended in complete failure.

The crowd was sympathetic, but even a friendly AA man could do nothing to help. We realised it was hopeless, so we gave up and returned to London.

Then a garage in Perth re-designed the Water Beetle, encasing the whole engine in a metal box. They also fitted two wave-breakers on the front, and a hand accelerator and two bilge pumps inside.

For our second attempt, we decided to leave from Port Patrick, a shorter crossing. When we arrived there, the Irish Sea didn't look at all friendly. In the morning our flotilla of support ships put to sea. The wind was very strong, and the support vessels were heaving

around in the heavy swell. I felt anxious as I watched the lumpy waves outside the bay. At the last moment, Steve couldn't be found, so I prepared to set off alone.

Steve finally appeared, and we were ready. As we drove into the sheltered waters of the bay, my confidence increased. The engine ran sweetly and the propeller whipped up the water into a white spray as we forged along. We checked the equipment before we left the bay, including the bilge pumps, the generator to charge our three batteries, and of course, the windscreen wipers!

Outside the bay the waves were much higher and there was a big rolling swell. The car wallowed badly as we climbed the crests of the waves and plunged into the troughs. The propeller dipped in and out of the water, the engine revved and screamed and spray crashed over the roof. The bilge pumps were working flat out but the interior seemed to fill up from everywhere — through the sun roof, the inside windows, the air vents. I was feeling very queasy when the message came over that we had done one mile. But now the battle against the tide and the rough sea was taking its toll of the engine and suddenly it stopped. After a couple of miles our second attempt now ended in failure.

Once again we were rescued by the lifeboat and the car was towed back to shore. The fault was discovered — the petrol cap hadn't been sealed, and water had seeped into the petrol tank. A waterproof seal was fitted, and the next morning, we were ready to try again.

This was our third and final attempt. The weather had improved slightly, but I felt even more nervous as we set off. I was not looking forward to being sick again, and to the huge waves which had smashed over the car on the previous day.

We followed the same procedures, and leaving the shelter of the bay we hit the rough tidal water. We spent our time checking the water level in the car, swapping the leads of the bilge pumps to fresh batteries and starting up the generator to re-charge the used batteries. The air in the car was thick and heavy; the only way we could breathe fresh air was by sticking our heads out of the sun roof. We got regular reports of our progress — after four hours we had come a third of the way across.

We had one or two unforeseen adventures. At one time the driver of the rescue boat rammed us quite severely, smashing Steve's side window and nearly pushing us over. Then a freak wave lifted us up and flicked us on our side. The water came pouring in through Steve's shattered window and the car filled up rapidly, but the bilge pumps managed to cope, and we were still afloat.

A nuclear submarine surprised us by surfacing about a mile away — no doubt to check out the unbelievable sight of a bright orange Beetle floating in the water! They circled round us to satisfy their curiosity before submerging.

We had covered about eleven miles when the waves began to get even bigger. The strong tide was sweeping us south into much rougher waters. Trouble started again, as our generator wasn't charging up the batteries properly. The bilge pumps were using up so much power that the current was being worn down too fast.

We had been going for eight hours now, and the seas were really heavy. We were taking on a lot of water, then the engine failed again. We just couldn't get it started because by now the batteries were quite flat. We prepared to abandon car and got ready for a tow.

We were both soaked and feeling very seasick as we boarded the rescue vessel. The Water Beetle was tied to the stern of the boat, and sank below the waves, the interior buoyancy keeping only a small part of the roof above the water.

It was a strange convoy that struggled into the harbour at Bangor, to be welcomed by a large crowd. Our cruiser was towing not only the submerged Water Beetle, but our trawler as well!

Left: Third time lucky? We're hoping that everything works this time.
Below: Abandon car! After eight hours the batteries fail and we're feeling very seasick.

Walking the tightrope is one of the most difficult and dangerous of all circus skills.

My instructor, Brian Androse, gave me my first lesson on the wire in his garden. This wire was only 18 inches off the ground, but Brian said that by the end of the day I would have a go on a six foot wire.

Brian then showed me how to stand on one leg and balance on the wire. I eventually managed to stand up, in a rather wobbly way. Further instructions followed: look straight ahead, arms out, body straight, bend your knees, concentrate. I finally made three steps but it was very difficult, like learning to walk all over again. After some time I began to control the wobbling, and was able to take a few more steps. Then I was right across in one go — what a triumph!

Now the real work began. The only way to improve was to practise, so Brian and I rigged up a wire in my back garden. He told me to stand on the wire every day for thirty minutes. Only after enough practice could I move up to a new height.

The weeks passed and gradually my confidence and skill increased, the wobbles disappeared and I could move, turn and balance on the wire with more ease. Then the day came when I was ready to practise in the circus for the first time. Here the wire was five feet high and had a different feel.

When I was more comfortable with the new wire, one of Brian's pupils, Bernie Bennett, taught me to use the long pole, and the lunge position. I found it incredibly difficult to balance, but Bernie told me to let the pole do the work of balancing. Eventually I managed it, but I couldn't imagine how I would do it on the high wire!

Over the next few weeks my act progressed considerably. I mastered one of the hardest feats for a tightrope walker, walking inside a bicycle wheel. Then one day Brian announced it was time to move to the high wire. The months of training had given me plenty of

TIGHTROPE

confidence on the low wire, but I was worried about going higher.

The first rule for any tightrope walker is to stay cool and relaxed. I tried to remember this as I nervously climbed the ladder. The high wire was about 13 feet above the ground and the first time across was the most difficult. It needed total concentration to keep my movements smooth and unhurried. I practised my tricks with the pole and the bicycle wheel, my mouth dry with fear. I knew that if I fell during the act I might seriously hurt myself.

I was to give my first performance in front of any audience on Sunday, April 14th 1985, a day I shall never forget. The crowds poured into Tamara Coco's Circus, while backstage I prepared myself for the walk of a lifetime. I dressed carefully, feeling very afraid, but I didn't want to fail. The show started, and Brian quietly talked to me, helping to control the panic welling up inside me. I was the last act, and had to wait for all the other acts to finish. This made me even more nervous. I felt like running away, but I couldn't back out now. The tension was unbearable.

Then suddenly I was announced: "The very daring . . . Peter Duncan", and I was out in the ring. I dropped my hat by mistake, took off my cloak, then slowly climbed up the ladder, my heart pounding. At the top I gave a cheery wave at the musical flourish, but I was far from feeling cheerful, and my stomach was churning at the thought of what I was about to do.

I took a deep breath, wiped the sweat from my eyes and picked up the pole. I stepped slowly onto the wire, not daring to think about the distance to the ground below. With intense concentration on every step I walked forward, placing my feet carefully on the wire. I was about a third of the way across when my nerve started to go and my knees started to tremble. I wobbled and began to lose balance, but I remembered my training, and kept going. I could feel the tension in the audience as I reached the middle of the wire. There I stopped to crouch, and the waves of applause reached up to me. I edged backwards along the wire and then, standing on one leg I balanced the pole carefully across my raised knee. The next part of the act was the lunge, which I performed cautiously. Then it was back to the safety of the platform.

Nerves quivering and legs shaking, I prepared to step out onto the wire again for the hardest part of the act, a complete walk without a harness or safety net, and my feet tangled up in a bicycle wheel. Gradually I edged forward, wobbling dangerously. Suddenly the wire shook, but with a great effort of will-power and concentration, I regained my balance and managed to finish my hazardous walk. The platform felt solid and stable as, trembling with relief, I stepped out of the hoop.

The audience applauded wildly as I clambered down to the ground, hardly able to stand from nervous reaction. Then I was out of the ring, feeling relieved and wildly exhilarated.

WALKER

Above: A burst of applause for my crouch, midway.
Left: The hardest part of the act – and no safety net!

DRAGON BOAT

Every year the ancient Chinese sport of Dragon Boat Racing draws teams from all over the world to compete in the international Dragon Boat Race in Hong Kong.

The technique in Dragon Boat racing is for the team to paddle following the beat of a drum. As the tempo of the drum beats increases, the paddles flash faster in and out of the water. In order to maintain a speed of thirty strokes, each crew member needs considerable strength and stamina. Would I be able to master this challenge, I wondered? I found co-ordination was a problem, and after a few runs, I was exhausted, but Jeff, the team leader, reckoned I was good enough to be in the team.

Then followed a period of intensive training in England. Concentration on the rhythm of the drum beat was all important to maintain a smooth arm stroke, and the muscles of my neck and arms complained at the long hours of training.

The day came when our training boat was put back into the boat house and we were on our way to Hong Kong. We were up against most of the Oriental teams who row about 80 strokes per minute and the best Chinese who row 90 a minute.

As dawn broke the next day the Chinese drummers settled the evil spirits to bring luck to the races. Our team found the rough waters of the Hong Kong harbour hard going.

Things weren't going too well for us to start with as our own timing was very ragged. Soon we managed to get more speed up, but disaster struck when a passing ship created such a swell that we shipped a lot of water and

began to sink. All hands had to abandon ship and to leap overboard. We were rescued by a passing sampan which managed to grab the camera being used to film us just in time.

On the day of the race, the big international race wasn't until the afternoon, but we decided to enter the first race of the day to see how fast we could go. The starting gun fired and the race was on. In out, in out, we seemed to go very fast, but even so, only made third place behind the top Chinese teams. However our time was amongst the fastest, and we had a good chance for the big race.

Teams from Harvard, Bangkok, Hong Kong, Germany and China meant we were up against the best in the world. The starter blared and we were off. We had to be in the first four to qualify for the final. Paddles flashed as we raced through the water. It was a photo finish between ourselves and Harvard — and then we heard we were in, the first British crew ever to get into the International Dragon Boat race final!

But then our luck changed. Drawn in lane eight, we were in the worst position. By now the heat and strain of the other two races were beginning to tell. As the race started, and the Chinese teams forged ahead, we just could not catch up. Still, we were well satisfied and it had been a great experience.

Left: The day of the race.
Above: Concentrating on the rhythm.

STUNT MAN

In action films, the most dangerous parts of the action are done by stunt men who take the place of actors. I decided to play James Bond in a Duncan Dares production based on *Diamonds are Forever*, but I would do all the stunts myself.

The opening sequence involved a beautiful girl, a fight with a Russian spy and a chase across the roof tops. The only escape from my villainous pursuer was a leap off the roof to the ground. It was now that I began to have my doubts — the ground looked very far off!

So the next day I got my first instructions from Tim Condren, the stunt co-ordinator. While a fall bed of padding was prepared, Tim explained the techniques of the fall and demonstrated how to land safely. When he jumped, it looked easy enough, rather similar to high diving, but the danger lay in twisting your neck if you landed awkwardly, or knocking your teeth out with your knees.

Then it was my turn to jump from the first stage onto the practice bed. I copied Tim and flipped over in the air, landing successfully on my back. My confidence increased and I climbed up quite happily to the next stage. It certainly looked higher when I was poised to jump, but on Tim's command, I let go and landed with a slightly harder thump. My heart was racing and I felt I had ricked my neck but mainly I was surprised at how much longer I seemed to be in the air.

I practised jumping from increasingly greater heights; every time I went up a few more rungs of the ladder, the stack seemed unbelievably far down. As my nervous tension built up, my confidence began to disappear, and it was not helped when Tim told me not to eat anything for five hours before the jump, in case I had to go to hospital!

As night fell, the stack of cushions was camouflaged to look like a pile of waste paper in a disused alleyway. I slowly climbed the ladder. Now it was all down to me.

Leaping off that roof was the most daring thing I did in the first series, because every instinct tells you not to do it. I had to concentrate hard on what I had to do. Slowly, I raised my arms, took a deep breath and hurled myself into space. Remembering Tim's instructions I flipped over and after what seemed an age — THUMP, I landed somewhat breathless and shaken, but still in one piece.

In the next scene I had to fight my way out of the alley. Doug Robinson, a judo expert, gave me advice on how to make the action look good. All the punches were carefully planned; it was like learning a sequence of steps in a dance — two punches, a side step, and swing. We rehearsed the whole sequence over and over again until the movements looked natural. The fight was filmed in the evening, and ended with me escaping in a car.

Then it was on to the next stunt, a high speed crash. First I had to learn the knack of jinking the steering wheel at the right time on a ramp so that the car rolls over. I felt quite confident about it beforehand, although Tim explained it requires discipline and training to get the car wheels correctly positioned on the ramp.

As night fell, wearing a crash helmet, I was strapped tightly into the car. My biggest fear was that something would come bursting

Below left: Making the action look good.
Below: Donning the fireproof suit, my special protective clothing.

through the windscreen into my face, or that I would rick my neck from the whip-lash effect of the impact.

Tim checked the car and then we were ready. This sort of stunt cannot be done twice, so seven cameras were used to film the action. Cardboard boxes hid the ramp to make it look as real as possible.

Then I was off. I slammed the accelerator to the floor, and as the car gathered speed, I concentrated on mounting the ramp in the exact position. Suddenly the ramp was in front of me and I jinked the wheel. The car crashed, nose over tail, clipping a lighting van in the process, before it slammed into the wall. Finally it came to rest, leaving me suspended upside down in the overturned car. It had felt like a horrifying dream sequence in slow-motion. I shall never forget the sensation of smashing glass and metal scraping against the ground, inches from my face.

In my final stunt, the car had to catch fire and I had to catch fire with it. Then I had to jump into the Thames to put out my burning clothes and wait for the divers to rescue me.

First I was dressed in a special fireproof suit with only my face left bare. Then I rehearsed my run a few times, feeling large and clumsy in my protective clothing. The danger was if I slipped and fell over, the flames would be around my face.

Tim smeared my back with inflammable gel, the car was set alight, and then it was my turn. I raced for the Thames, with flames billowing from my back and legs. Pausing a second on the embankment, I leaped in. The flames were suddenly quenched, and I was pulled out of the water. Once again I had escaped unharmed.

Below: As the car explodes, I race for the Thames, flames billowing. Only seconds to lose!

SURVIVAL

Lofty Wiseman specialises in survival techniques, so I decided to learn from him how to survive on my own in the wild for seven days. My first location was by a remote lake in Herefordshire. From here I planned my route to civilisation and survival.

Lofty chose a likely looking spot, sheltered from the winds, for my home in the forest. Our first task was to make my shelter. I cut a pile of saplings while Lofty made the framework. We thatched the frame with bracken, and I gathered armfuls of bracken for my bed.

We then made a fire. I collected firewood, and Lofty showed me how to make kindling. I struck my flint with the knife which produced sparks and ignited the cotton wool. We gradually added dry twigs until the fire was burning up merrily.

Lofty then suggested I fetch some water. I went to the lake to fill my tin can and when I returned to camp, I found he had built a trestle to hang the can over the fire. We boiled the water well, then Lofty passed me the can. I thought it would taste like dirty pond water, but it was warm and pleasant.

We then made a sleeping bag from eight panels of a parachute which we pretended I'd landed with. Lofty cut the cloth to make a bag I could sleep in.

By this time I was feeling pretty hungry, having only had boiled water all day. I made a makeshift rod with a little twig as a float, and put a fat grub on the hook. "Tight lines", Lofty wished me as I set off for the lake. Tight lines meant lots of fish! Before dark, we also put out my night lines — rope attached to a stone with three or four hooks on.

Dusk had fallen by now and I was grateful for the heat of the fire, although my eyes were smarting and my stomach craved food. That

Opposite: We choose a likely spot.
Left: Making the shelter (top).
The fire's alight, at last (middle).
Survival can be a miserable business . . .

first night I felt quite peaceful and content as I stared into the flames. The forest had come alive, with the wind creaking in the trees, and strange rustlings in the undergrowth, but I was quite tired and with a last sip of boiled water, I was soon asleep.

I woke at first light to find my fire had gone out, but I lit it again, and boiled up more water. Hunger was now becoming an obsession, so on Lofty's return the first thing we did was to forage around to find some edible plants. At the lake Lofty pulled up some bulrushes. We scrubbed the mud off the roots and Lofty showed me how to peel them down to the white flesh. We collected stinging nettles, camomile for tea and maiden fern and headed back to the camp.

We put the strange ingredients into my can and boiled the water. After some minutes, my meal was ready. I speared a root with a twig and carefully chewed an end. It was really quite good, so I went on to try the cooked nettle leaves and other ingredients. Later I found I had caught two small fish on my night lines which I cooked over the fire. Their flavour was amazing, and I swallowed them down hungrily.

As part of my plan to be rescued we had to swim across the lake. I felt uncooperative with a nagging headache. We undressed and stuffed our clothes into plastic bags, then I followed Lofty into the muddy water. It was freezing, and I really felt rotten. We swam to the other shore and clambered out. Our bags had kept our clothes dry, and the dip in the water had livened me up. I began to feel better as we dressed and sat in the sunshine.

It was now time to see how well I had learned to survive. Lofty wished me "Tight lines", and left me by myself. I worked hard at my various jobs. I caught a larger fish, foraged for food and collected firewood. That night the weather changed and it was cold and damp.

The wind gusted through the trees and I really felt close to the earth as smoke swirled around my shelter, and sparks flew about.

The next day I found my fire had gone out and that I had lost my flint. I was in a real panic until I found another flint. The weather had brightened, and having got my fire going, there was more fishing and wood collecting to do. Because of lack of food, my energy had slowed down, so that afternoon, I had a long sleep. I was now very familiar with my surroundings and felt I'd been here for weeks. With no possessions and no worries, I liked my simple pattern of living.

On the third night I needed some water and wandered down to the lake in the dark. When I heard the sound of heavy breathing, my heart leapt into my mouth. Who or what could it be? To my amazement I found it was a hedgehog, panting in a very human fashion. I was unnerved by this experience and quickly climbed back into my makeshift sleeping bag.

Lofty arrived in the morning, and we shared a can of camomile tea. Then it was time to break camp and move to our next location. Lofty showed me how to make a simple rucksack and I packed my few belongings. We scattered the embers of the fire, and with my rucksack on my back, I said goodbye with some regret to my little home in the woods.

I now had a 12 mile walk over the Brecon Beacons. Lofty led the way, carrying a large pack with safety gear. To start off the weather was pleasantly cool, but as the cloud base lowered, visibility was reduced to almost nothing. Soon I was soaked through to the skin from the rain and the bogs I had fallen into, and was beginning to feel very fed up. My feet were sore and my boots rubbed my heels.

Lofty chose a camp site by a pine forest, with a waterfall nearby which thundered down onto the rocks. We made a poncho shelter, a single flat water proof sheet pegged at an angle to some rocks. I was depressed and exhausted. My ankle hurt and the blisters on my feet were very painful so Lofty treated them with potassium permanganate. When he had finished, my feet were covered in lurid purple blotches, but they felt better.

I built a fire and had a meagre meal of fish, and a few broad beans. That night I had very little sleep, the noise of the waterfall was so loud. Eventually I could stand it no longer, so stuffing some cotton wool in my ears, I stuck my socks under my hat to muffle the sound. With my head buried in my sleeping bag, I eventually managed to drop off.

Next day we broke camp again. I was very pleased to leave my primitive mountain lodging. I had to do another long trek to see how I would cope with physical stress. On the way, Lofty found some tiny wild strawberries which were delicious. He showed me how to scrape the root free of dirt, and rub it across my teeth to remove plaque. So I cleaned my teeth for the first time in six days!

Then we came to a step-sided quarry which I had to scramble up. I felt much weaker now from lack of food, and only just managed to drag myself over the top on my hands and knees.

That night I set up another poncho shelter between two trees. The weather was atrocious and my spirits were at their lowest ebb as I sat and watched the rain pour down. Everything was damp — the wood, the ground and the clothes I had been wearing for the last six days. I couldn't be bothered to try and dry them out, and just crawled into my sleeping bag.

Left: Lovely to look at, but far too noisy at night. Eventually, I manage to nod off . . .
Below: foraging for food – stinging nettles, ferns, bulrushes, I eat the lot. It even tastes good!

Top right: Fire is a vital part of survival. Without kindling, I might come to grief.

The next day Lofty found out I had no kindling left and only four pieces of damp firewood. He said that I really would come to grief if I didn't sort myself out, but by this time I no longer cared that I was breaking all the rules for survival by not having the means to make a fire.

We trudged on and finally came to the coast. We scrambled over the rocks, and Lofty pointed out all the food available. We filled my can with mussels, whelks, cockles, barnacles, and bladderwort, an edible seaweed. Finally I prised some limpets off the rocks. We built a fire, and boiled up the contents of the can. It was the strangest concoction, but it was the first proper meal I had eaten for seven days and it was delicious.

In my final bid to escape to civilisation we built a raft from oil drums and bits of timber. We made the base from a huge spar, attached the oil drums, then all we had to do was to wait for the tide to come in. When the waves were swirling around my feet I tried to balance on the raft, but a big wave knocked me over. The raft smashed against the rocks and broke up — it was a disaster.

By now we felt we had come to the end of my adventure. We built one last fire as a beacon for passing ships but all I could think of was a hot bath and a cup of tea.

FIREMAN

Before I could go on duty as a fireman I had to have some basic training at Southwark Training Centre and a day with the river police. I was fitted out in my fireman's clothes and assigned to a group of other recruits.

First we learnt the 'carry down' which involved rescuing somebody by ladder from the fourth floor of a building. The problem is the top of the ladder is quite narrow and you go down using opposite hands and feet for each

rung. The person I was carrying weighed 150 lbs, so it was a real strain to bring him to the ground safely. I nearly gave up at the last few rungs, but managed to reach the bottom.

My hands were blistered and I felt exhausted, but it was on to the next project where we had to go up inside a water tower to put a fire out. We rolled out the fire hoses and connected them to the fire-engine. They were then charged up with water, making them very firm and hard to bend. To get this awkward long pipe round right-angled corners 50-60 times is not easy. As Number 3 and a new member of the team, I was not much help. Numbers 1 and 2 held the nozzle of the hose, and I relayed their messages down the tower, and fed them the hose as it was pushed up to me. By the twelfth floor I was shattered, but I was not allowed to rest. When we reached the top of the tower, the water was turned off, and we had to take the hose back down the stairs, squeeze out the water, disconnect the sections and roll them up again before stowing them back on the fire-engine. As the novice, I was lumbered with rolling up three hoses!

I learned to operate the breathing apparatus. You wear a heavy cylinder on your back, and a mask which covers your face and nose. The seal of the mask must be airtight, so I had to have my hair cut, as otherwise my hair would break the seal.

When you enter a building on fire, you go in threes and keep in contact with the next man, shouting instructions from one to another. Each man has a number, and I was Number 2. We had to enter a smoke-filled room to retrieve a body which we had to carry through a complicated structure of tunnels. Number 1 went in, staying in touch with the wall, and we others followed him, holding hands to keep in contact. The first thing I found was the sofa; Number 3 hit a chair, and then I found the body. It weighed 176 lbs and the head came off when I picked it up, so I left that behind and dragged the rest out into the

Opposite: All dressed up and raring to go, I'm ready for action.

Left: Feeling part of the team, I help to extinguish the flames.
Below: On the Thames with the river police, in training.

tunnel. By now I was feeling exhausted and was pouring with sweat.

We just managed to get through the tunnel by pushing and pulling at the body. I was really struggling by then and when we checked the air in our cannisters, I found I had used much more than the other two because of my high panic level.

After my training, on November 5th I went on duty with the night shift of a fire station. As I drove up, the alarm bell went off and I was soon in the fire engine racing down Holloway Road. This first call was to some flats where a young man had got stuck in a lift. We had to use a crowbar to get him out.

Back at the fire station, I was just having a cup of tea when the alarm went again. We raced to a local estate, and found we had to deal with a street fire. I pulled out the hose and helped put the fire out.

We had just started to serve up our dinner when the alarm went yet again. This time it was a fire on a garage roof. I was put in charge of putting out the fire and really began to feel part of the team.

TRUCK

Truck racing is a relatively new sport in England and the idea of hurtling round a circuit at about 100 mph in a huge 7–ton truck was quite a challenge. But a lot of preliminary training was necessary, as I had never driven a truck before.

I borrowed a Roadtrain from British Leyland's T45 race team and went to Brand's Hatch to meet the team manager, Horace Jessop, and be introduced to my truck. Horace took me through the gear box which, unlike a car, has 13 speeds and sounded very complicated.

My first problem was the seat which had to be moved right forward. Turning on the engine, I could feel the power under the bonnet. I went on a trial run around the circuit and found it unnerving as I carefully drove round the course with other trucks continuously hurtling past me. It was difficult to navigate round the corners in the right gear, but Horace told me that I would improve with practice.

Then it was off to the Thames Valley training school at Abingdon to learn to drive a truck properly. After five days intensive training, I was ready to take the test for a HGV licence which I needed for truck racing. I was a bag of nerves when I finished the test, and could hardly believe it when the instructor said I had passed! I was now able to get my competitor's licence and we were all set for racing in the French Truck Grand Prix at the Paul Ricard circuit in the south of France.

We arrived there on the Wednesday evening before the race. As I watched the trucks hurtling around the track and met some of the other drivers, I realised what a challenge I had let myself in for.

We persuaded the organisers to allow me some unofficial practice on the track in the morning so that I could learn about the truck and the circuit without other racers breathing down my neck. I climbed up into the cab and Horace explained that I could check my time round each lap as he would chalk it up on a board for me to see. I set off and did a couple

RACER

of gentle circuits. Then one of the British drivers, Mel Bacon, took the Roadtrain round to show me what it was capable of. As Mel threw the truck round each bend at speed, I realised how far I had to go before I would be competitive.

In the afternoon I had further instruction from Mel, and then was on my own. Now there were other trucks practising on the track, but by the end of the day, I had developed more speed and confidence. I still had trouble with the sixth gear so the engineers checked the gearbox. They soon discovered that it was the driver who was at fault!

I practised all day, hurtling round the corners, spinning off the track and curling round back onto it, learning how, when I lost control on a corner, I could drive into the turn and correct the fault. I had a couple of minor crashes, but was finding out what to do if I got into trouble, and how to control the truck under speed and pressure.

The following day there was an official practice session which was timed. This, together with a final practice session on

Left: Meeting my truck for the first time. Even the gear box is a challenge.
Above: Out on the racing circuit, I'm limbering up for the competition.

Saturday morning, would decide my place on the grid at the start of the race. Horace and the mechanics checked my speed, which by Saturday morning had improved until I was lapping at 2 minutes 4 seconds, only 7 seconds behind the leaders.

Before the race my tyres were checked and the worn ones replaced. After a final engine check, I donned my crash helmet, Horace locked the safety bar into position, and I drove out to take up my position on the track.

My starting position on the grid was third from the rear. There were about 17 other trucks in the race, which was for the most powerful models. The race started by a warm-up lap in formation, then the leader truck disappeared into the pits, and we were off into the first bend. Being towards the back, it was like plunging into a dark chasm filled with diesel oil and smoke; I couldn't see a thing. Trucks seemed to be everywhere, spinning off and crashing into the side of the bend. I managed to avoid the obstacles and get through to the long fast back straight. I held my position ahead of the other two trucks, but now I was faced with the problem of passing a Frenchman in an orange truck that I had caught up with. It took me two laps to make up my mind, then I powered past him on the back straight, cut in again to the main track and was ahead of him.

The Frenchman in turn put on the pressure, following closely on my tail. On the fifth lap I swung into a tight right-hand bend, but couldn't find the right gear to drive out of it. To my horror, the Roadtrain spun round and hurtled into the crash barrier in reverse. The truck was on the point of tipping over as it came to rest with the rear wheels high on the safety tyres lining the track. I stamped on the throttle and the huge truck surged forward, scattering rubber tyres behind me as it spun round to face the right way and I headed off in pursuit of the field.

Unfortunately I had to retire one lap later because the accelerator got jammed to the floor. I got out of the truck and was marshalled across the track, to be confronted by all the British drivers, who praised my attempt to carry on after the crash. I was only sad that I didn't finish the race.

The second race the next day was just as exciting, if less eventful. By this time, I was feeling exhausted from the strain and nervous tension of the previous days. I battled for position with three other trucks and finished in ninth place.

Opposite: In the first race, I finally summon up courage to overtake!
Top: Hurtling into the crash barrier – backwards!
Above: Rejoining the race – the right way round.
Left: They give you a cup, even when you come ninth!

CLIMBER

On the west coast of Scotland is a sea stack called the Old Man of Stoer, which juts out from the coast like a jagged tooth. This was the scene of one of the most hazardous dares I attempted. With my friend Doug Scott, one of the world's best mountaineers, I was to scramble up the 250 feet of vertical rock face.

Before we could start the adventure, we had to descend the cliff face and cross the seven-metre wide channel to the base of the stack. We had a rope handrail to help us, and as we got lower, we came across a strange phenomenon. It looked like snow, but a small speck which landed in my eye confirmed it was something more unpleasant — detergent. This offensive pollution was to cause me considerable problems during the climb.

Once at the bottom of the cliff, Doug explained I had to swim across the channel with a rope around my waist, and he would follow by pulling himself across on the rope. As I looked anxiously at the seething water, Doug cheerily pointed out an enormous jellyfish, and a bull seal watching nearby, but there was no other way across. I stripped down to my underpants, and judging the moment, dived in. The freezing water took my breath away, but once I had got over the

Below: Doug Scott and me on the cliff-top.

Left: The Old Man of Stoer.
Below: Scaling the rock face.

shock, I swam as fast as I could and just made it to the other side before a big wave pounded onto the rocks.

I found a sheltered ledge and made the rope fast for Doug to swing across with the equipment and my clothes. Soon he was explaining the bits of tackle and how to rope up for the climb. I particularly liked the metal chocks called 'friends', which when jammed into cracks in the rock, could hold a person's weight.

We were ready to go, and Doug explained that we would divide the climb into sections called 'pitches'. Doug was to lead the climb, except for the last pitch. I gazed up at the rock

face — I was going to need as many 'friends' as possible, I thought.

Doug made short work of the first pitch. Then it was my turn. I tried to remember where he had put his hands and feet, but I felt very clumsy and awkward as I set out. The swirling clouds of detergent didn't help, as they made the rock face very slippery and stung my eyes and face. I was wearing a safety helmet, and that, and the crashing of the waves on the rocks below, prevented me from hearing Doug's advice. I felt very nervous as I groped for hand and toe holds. Gradually I inched my way up the rock face. As I drew nearer Doug's encouragement gave me more confidence, and I relaxed a little.

My confidence was short-lived however, as the next pitch was one of the trickier parts. There was an overhanging section, and Doug had stressed the need to lean out at this point, but I found myself desperately hugging the rock face, unable to move. Doug was out of sight, and I felt very alone and vulnerable. Try as I would, I didn't have the nerve to reach out over the bulge. In the end I just went for it and scrabbled my way up until I found a little ledge where I could rest. My heart was pounding and I felt quite giddy when I looked down at the waves swirling over the rocks below. However when I set off again, I felt sure that nothing about me could be as bad, and I began to think I might actually reach the top.

I found the next pitch a bit easier, but the fourth pitch had another problem, a vertical crack in the rocks called a chimney. Doug told me to climb inside it, leaning my back against one wall and edging my feet up the other. I couldn't manage such a difficult manoeuvre and found myself stuck again. I was getting tired and my energy was beginning to flag. In a panic I shouted up to Doug "I can't do it." "Yes you can", came his calm reply, and I did.

The wind was now much stronger; we had a little rest and I began to feel quite excited as I realised we were now just below the summit. It was now my turn to lead the final pitch. We changed over ropes and very cautiously, I led off. I went slowly, without looking down, and came to a final difficult move not far from the top. As I was working out how to overcome the obstacle, I saw the helicopter circling the summit to take close-ups of me. This did not

Left: *We make it to the top. After five hours, it's exhilarating – a real achievement!*

help, as I was not sure whether to look at the helicopter, or to concentrate on the rock face. Then I was up and over the obstruction, and I was at the summit. I'd reached the top after five hours of gruelling climbing.

I waved to the helicopter and an overwhelming feeling of exhilaration swept over me. Soon Doug was standing beside me. I could not stop grinning at him, the sense of achievement was so wonderful, and I could tell he was equally delighted.

Up to then, I really hadn't thought about getting off the stack. Doug's plan sounded terrifying. A steel wire was set up between the top of the rock and the edge of the cliff and I had to pull myself hand over hand along its length. By now I was very tired and it took me three-quarters of an hour to reach the other side. It was only when I was sitting on the cliff top that we realised that the screws on the carabenas which had supported me had come undone. One awkward turn, and that might have been it, a sickening plunge to the rocks below.

Above: A terrifying plan that only just works . . . inching along the steel wire, high above the rocks.

I DARE YOU TO...

Bed of Nails, Python and Tarantula

For the second series of Duncan Dares, I asked Blue Peter viewers to suggest some gruesome things for me to do. One letter was from Keira Lindsey, who dared me to lie on a bed of nails holding a snake, with a tarantula crawling across my chest.

This sounded pretty horrible, so I went to see Trevor, who specialises in bed of nail acts. I found him filing down the points of the nails, which were 5 ins long, and felt pretty sharp already!

Trevor explained that to lie on a bed of nails you spread your weight as evenly as possible, but even so, it would be painful. Trevor's own act was to lie on the bed of nails with an 18 stone man standing on his chest — but I was to have a 16 foot long python instead.

Trevor told me that pythons were not poisonous, but they can wrap themselves round you and crush you to death. This was not very encouraging, especially when he explained that pythons have about 300 very small teeth and that when they bite, they don't just grip, but they bite deep into the flesh and if you try to pull away, they can rip your hand or arm off.

Then Trevor and his assistant brought out Monty to meet me. The python was so huge it needed both of them to carry it. Monty looked at me with unblinking eyes, his tongue flickering in and out. I touched him very gently; his skin was cold, but dry and smooth. I shuddered to think of him slithering over me.

I was then introduced to the tarantula. Trevor was terrified of spiders and kept at a safe distance as the huge red-kneed tarantula

was brought out. Tarantulas are not poisonous, so thinking I ought to handle her before the act, I gently took the creature onto my palm. It was rather like holding a soft bath sponge, and quite safe as long as I did not frighten her. Trevor refused to touch her, and he was quite relieved when I returned the tarantula to her keeper.

I was to be one of the acts to appear in the circus that evening. When it was time for my act, the bed of nails was shown to the audience, then Monty was carried into the ring, to horrified gasps from the audience. I lay down gently on the bed of nails and felt them dig into my skin. It was really painful,

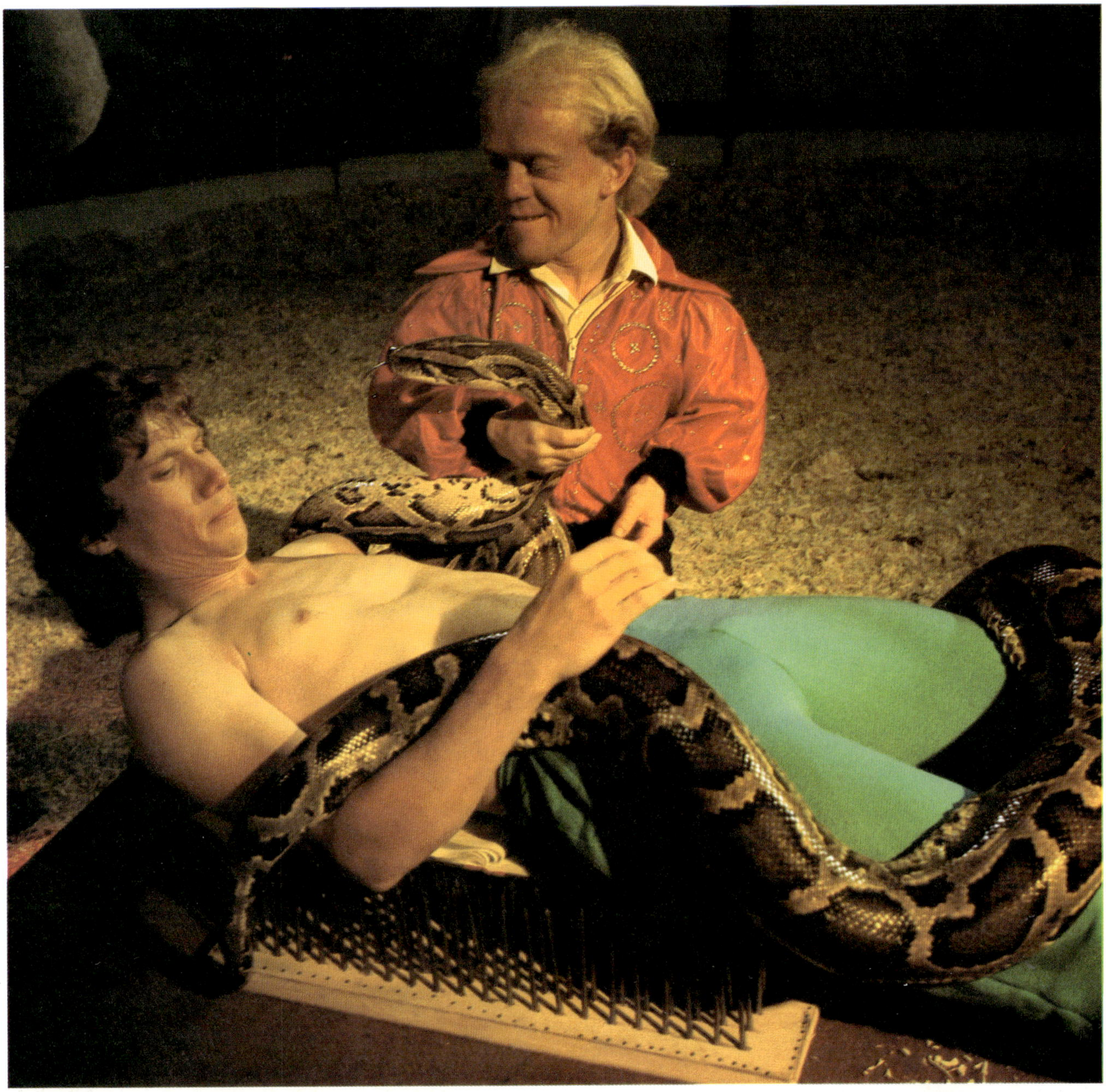

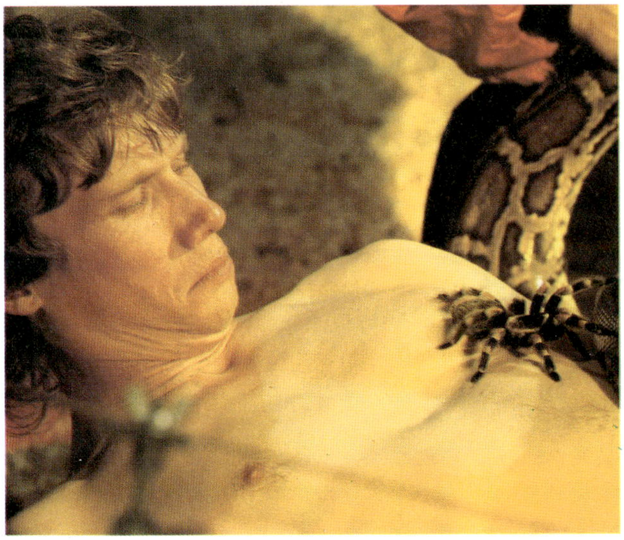

but worse was to follow. Trevor gently draped Monty over my body and his coils wrapped around me. Trevor was being very careful with Monty's head, as he was worried about the reaction of the python to the tarantula.

I hardly dare breathe when finally the tarantula was placed on my bare chest. To my horror it began to crawl up towards my face. As one furry leg was about to step onto my chin, it was whisked away just in time. The audience, who had watched in morbid fascination, clapped and cheered. Then Monty was at last removed from my crumpled body. Gently I uncurled from the bed of nails; the indentures where the nails had been throbbed with a vengeance.

Beard of Bees

To bee or not to bee?

My next adventure came from Fiona Barker, who dared me to wear a beard of bees. I went to Hazel Street Bee Farm in Kent to find out what a beard of bees is. There I met Ken Beaver, the bee-farmer, who appeared unconcerned by the thousands of bees flying all around him, although the film crew were well protected by masks and gowns!

Ken explained that a beard of bees is a swarm of bees on your chin, with the queen bee in the centre and the other bees making a beard below the chin as they settle around her. I asked anxiously how safe it was, and was not reassured when Ken laughed and said that even a bee-keeper wouldn't like to do it!

I remembered when I had been stung as a little boy and shuddered as Ken scooped up a handful of bees and offered them to me. Somehow I held out my hand, and Ken gently shook the bees onto it. I dared not look at them, as I stood rigid with fear, with bees crawling over my hand and up my arm. Ken explained that all the bees had their stings in them, and I would certainly know it if I got stung! The trick is not to yell or jump about, otherwise they'd sting me, and then I'd be in real trouble.

Ken then explained how we make the beard. The queen bee was placed in a small plastic cage which I had to suspend from my mouth by a string. The other bees would then be attracted to the queen and form the beard.

Ken first caught the queen, and placed her in the plastic cage with great care. Then he hung the cage in the hive to let the other bees know where their queen was.

After a time the cage was completely covered with bees, and Ken gave me the string from which the cage was hanging. I slowly raised the string to my lips, but at the first attempt my courage failed — I could not bring the beard up to my face. I tried again and this time got the end of the string in my mouth. The sound of hundreds of bees buzzing around my face was like a nightmare. Then I felt them begin to settle on my neck and chin. Ken told me to raise my head so that the beard touched my chin as he scooped up more bees to join the swarm. I closed my eyes as the beard grew and grew. Bees seemed to be everywhere, but finally the torture was ended. Ken ran out of bees and the beard was removed — and I had not been stung once!

Knaresborough Bed Race

The official BBC Radio York bed-racing team.

The next letter I received was a dare from Judith Harrison to join in the Knaresborough Bed Race, an international event drawing teams from all over Europe. I would be part of the BBC Radio York team. Judith explained the hazards of the demanding course. She would sit in the middle of our customized bed frame, while five strapping lads and myself would push her round the route. The demanding course included cobbled streets, steep hills and a long descent to the river.

The variety and style of beds was amazing, ranging from a hi-tech German bed made of light aluminium, to a Victorian four-poster. My team discovered the knack of keeping our bed on the move, but had to slow down to almost a walk going uphill. Going down the steep slope on the other side was not much easier, as the bed almost escaped from our clutches. We raced after it and just managed to get it under control before we reached the river. We plunged in, and I was soon out of my depth. We'd attached a couple of plastic containers to make the bed bouyant, and with the help of ropes we pulled it across. Then we had to heave it up the bank, slipping and sliding on the grass and mud. A few more metres and we had crossed the finishing line. Our team had made it in 20.29 minutes, which was well down the field, but Judith was happy, and she did promise to write to someone else if she had any more crazy ideas.

Seal Cave

My next dare was from Mitch Adams in Cornwall, who dared me to enter a hidden cavern where a colony of seals live. As we dived off the boat with our safety guide Robin, an inquisitive bull seal surfaced to watch us. He soon disappeared however, and we swam for the shore. The water was clear and very cold and the current tugged us as we reached the rocks and saw the jagged cleft in the cliff which led to the seals' cave. It looked dark and forbidding, and I wondered what we would find inside.

The channel narrowed quickly and soon we were swimming in the dark with the heavy swell surging against the rocks on either side. The lamps on our safety helmets were our only light and their weak beam did not penetrate very far. Our voices echoed as we swam deeper into the cave — where were the seals, I wondered?

Then I felt soft sand under my feet and we clambered out onto a beach. I flashed a torch around. The cave was enormous and led back into the cliffs. We found a buoy from the fishing nets which had been washed into the cave by a storm — perhaps the seals used it to play football with!

As we sat down to sip some welcome mugs of hot chocolate, I asked Robin where all the seals were. He said that they had probably heard us entering the cave, and rushed down the beach to escape. This explained all the scuff marks on the beach, but it seemed odd to think that the seals had been swimming below us when we were swimming on the surface!

Then it was time to return to the daylight which beckoned at the distant mouth of the cave. We put on our flippers and struck out for the entrance. The water surged in and out of the cave and it was a hard swim back. We were glad to emerge into the bright sun and see the boat waiting for us just off shore.

Send in the seals!

Firewalk

My next dare from Martyn Jones was far more nerve-wracking. Martin dared me to walk barefoot over a bed of red hot coals.

This is not the sort of stunt you do without really expert tuition, so Dr David Dean, a veteran firewalker, was in charge of my attempt.

We built a huge fire in a field and Martin helped me pile logs on the flames. The heat built up until the coals had reached a temperature of 650 degrees C.

The heat was fierce and as I looked at the red hot embers, I could imagine the pain of my burning feet and my courage deserted me. I practised with David the number of steps I would take over the bed of coals. The key was to relax my body.

The coals glowed an evil red in the dark as I stood in front of them. I drew a deep breath and walked forwards, but I stopped at the edge. I couldn't go any further. Backing off, I tried to conquer my fear. All my instincts told me not to do it, yet somehow I knew that if I did it correctly, I would not be hurt. Suddenly I surprised myself as I took four slow, measured steps across the glowing embers. Then I was over, with my feet on the cool wet grass being sprayed with cold water. I had done it! A feeling of relief swept over me, and I had escaped with only minor blisters on the soles of my feet.

Later I found it easier to repeat the trick, and with a little encouragement it was also done by producer Rob Benfield.

Cold feet? Who, me?

COMMANDO

Before young Royal Marine recruits win their green berets, their final test is a speed march or yomp across some of the roughest country in Britain. You need to be fit, but you also need courage and confidence to overcome hours of pain and exhaustion.

My preparations for the yomp began with a combined tarzan and assault course carrying full kit, to be completed in 12 minutes. I did it more than once and my best time came close, but I wasn't wearing the heavy webbing that I would have for the yomp.

The next day, Troop Commander Fred Simpson took me for a speed march wearing the webbing. He wanted to check me out, because the 30 mile yomp is the ultimate Commando test and a strain even for the fit young recruits.

In a speed march there is not a lot of marching. Speed is important, so you spend most of the time running.

On the day before the yomp, we assembled for our briefing. I was assigned to the first syndicate. The run was to take place on Dartmoor, from Okehampton Battle Camp in the north to Scout Hut Wood on the southern edge of the moor.

Late that afternoon we joined the coach which took us to Okehampton. After our arrival, we unpacked, then settled down to discuss the route. The troop weren't as worried as I was about the physical test of endurance. They were more concerned about the huge Dartmoor bogs which could swallow a man without trace.

Fred gave us a few survival tips, which included putting plaster on our chests to avoid 'jogger's nipple', and Vaseline between

Yomping. The ultimate Commando test . . .

YOMP

our toes, under the armpits and in the groin, to stop friction. He said we would get very wet, not only from the mist and rain, but from our own sweat.

At the final briefing that evening I had a nasty surprise. As the troop were all carrying rifles, they said it was only fair that I should carry an orange crook of equal weight.

It was still dark when we woke up next morning. The rain was cascading down. After a big breakfast we marched to the start with 8 hours to complete the course.

The first stage was up a gentle incline. Soon the fast pace set by the syndicate left me trailing behind. In the cold light of dawn the gale blew into my face and the rain soaked my webbing. The heavy webbing meant that I kept falling behind. Arriving at Checkpoint 1, I was about half a mile behind them.

When my syndicate reached Checkpoint 2, they were a good 10 minutes behind schedule, but I was another 20 minutes behind them.

By now I was in a fairly bad state. I was pale with fatigue as I staggered wearily up to the Checkpoint. I was told that I had no hope of completing the march, but it was decided that I would be allowed to continue the next stage. My feet felt fine, but by now the crook was rubbing the centre of my back.

Checkpoint 3 offered hot soup and pasties to the recruits. I was beginning to feel better with my second wind. I was determined to get to the end, and put on an air of cheerfulness and confidence. Captain Smith reported on my performance on the last stage. Fred reluctantly agreed to take me on the next leg, to the forest end at Hexworthy.

It was nearly 2 o'clock when I struggled into Checkpoint 4. I had tried to put on a final spurt to persuade them to let me go on to the finish, but by now I was weakening and I knew from their faces it was no good.

I was disappointed not to have finished the whole course, but the recruits all made it, and were awarded their coveted green berets.

HANG GLIDER

For this dare it was decided that having learnt to hang-glide, I would fly across the Channel to France and deliver the mail.

I started my instruction at Steyning, and having put the hang-glider together, began my lesson at the bottom of the hill. I ran and lifted off the ground and although my teacher, Kelvin, would not let me go too high, I found it exhilarating. We did a number of runs and I managed to control the glider, each time going higher up the hill, doing longer runs and rising up a little bit higher in the air.

I also learned how to land, although I occasionally got tangled up in the harness.

After a time my shoulders started to ache, but by the end of the first day I had managed one good 76 yards flight.

We filmed my first flight from the top of Devil's Dyke, and I was to do a second flight, with the cameras at the bottom of the hill, to show the landing. This proved impossible, as a sea breeze came in and the wind direction changed. I couldn't take off in this cross wind and they hadn't filmed me landing. When they tried to simulate a landing, I had my first real accident. The film crew pulled me along the ground on a long rope to lift me in the air, but I veered to the left and plummeted into the ground with a real thump.

Ready to go, take-off . . . and an unscheduled watery landing!

Our plan was that having learned to fly I should be winched up to 9000 feet on a wire for my cross Channel flight. I hadn't gained enough air time to succeed on my own, so it was decided that I should go dual, with Graham Deegan as my partner in this historic flight. The problem was that to cross the Channel, the wind and weather had to be very specific to make the flight a success. In addition I had to get a lot of winch training in, and time was running out.

When you crash a hang-glider into water, it can be fatal. Graham and I were anxious about this, and wanted to practice getting out of our harness under water. We were worried that we might hit the water out of control or be entangled in the parachute if we had an emergency. We went to Hastings, where we were to leap off the harbour wall to see if we could get out. The results were horrendous. Graham went first and was very shaken up. He was under water for about 15 seconds but didn't unclip himself. Then it was my turn. I hit the water in a strange way, nose first, and it dragged me right into the back of the wing. I was struggling to swim forward in the harness, but couldn't, and was under water for 23 seconds. I probably had about 5 seconds left before I would have my lungs filled with water. When I came out, I was determined there was no way I would do that again!

Having done that practice, we went to the Isle of Wight for our big take off. We only had to get up to about 5000 feet to get across the Solent. But again it was a terrible failure. The wire kept on getting caught in the sand and it kept twisting and breaking. We had one abortive flight where we got up to 50 feet and came down with a big thump on the ground.

We contacted Judy Leden, the women's world champion hang-glider, to be my partner.

As we go to print, our plan is that Judy Leden and I will attempt to break the dual hang-gliding record together by soaring along ridges in Wales, if the weather is kind. By the time you read this, maybe you will know if we made it!